D0853264

# CASEY

## The Utterly Impossible Horse

# CASEY
## The Utterly Impossible Horse

### A STORY BY ANITA FEAGLES

With Illustrations By Dagmar Wilson

Young Scott Books

Text Copyright © 1960 by Anita MacRae Feagles
All Rights Reserved
A Young Scott Book
Addison-Wesley Publishing Company, Inc.
Reading, Massachusetts 01867
Library of Congress Card Catalog No. 60-50242
ISBN: 0-201-09149-6
Printed in the United States of America

EFGHIJK-WZ-7987

## Mike Meets Casey

Mike got off the school bus with a lot of other children, but he didn't walk home with any of them because he wanted to see if he could find some good rocks for his rock collection.

So nobody was with him when he saw the horse.

The horse was just standing there, and Mike

was surprised because he had never seen a horse anywhere near his house before.

Mike got up out of the ditch, where he'd been looking for rocks, and went over to the horse.

"Hello, horsie. Where did you come from?" he asked.

"Well," the horse said, "I was just here, waiting for the school bus."

"Hey! Was that you talking?" Mike asked.

"Of course," the horse said. "You don't see any other horse around, do you?"

"Well, no," Mike said.

The horse bent over to eat some grass. Finally Mike said, "I didn't know horses could talk, though."

"Have you ever talked to a horse?"

"No," Mike said.

"Well, then," the horse said.

Mike wondered what he meant by that remark, but he waited awhile and then he said, "Why were you waiting for the school bus?"

"I was hoping some boy would take me home to live with him. You see, I don't have a boy."

"Golly, I'd sure like you to come live with me, but we don't have a barn, or anything like that. Nobody around here does."

"A garage will be all right."

"Really? You mean you'll come live with me, and be my own horse?"

"No. *You'll* be *my* boy."

"Sure, in a way," Mike said. "Will my mother be surprised!"

"Oh, I never talk to grownups."

"My mother won't mind that," Mike said. "In fact, I think she'd just as soon you didn't. Wow! I have a horse!" Mike shouted.

"What's your name?" the horse asked.

"Mike Bradford. And I have a big sister, Gloria, and my mother and father. What's your name?"

The horse thought a minute. "I guess my name will be Mike."

"But that's *my* name!"

"Don't you like it?"

"Sure, but—gee whiz, I'd feel funny calling you Mike."

"All right, then. My name will be Gloria."

"That's my sister's name. Besides, it's for a girl. Don't you like any other names?"

"Well," the horse said, "You certainly are fussy. Let me see. I know. My name will be Mr. Bradford."

"Oh, come on," Mike said. "That's my father's name. You can't have that name."

The horse started looking around. "I guess I'll find another boy."

"No, listen, horsie—"

"And I don't like to be called horsie. There must be some other boy."

"Come on, please. Listen, you can have any other name in the whole world. I mean, not Mrs. Bradford, either, but any other name. I promise."

"Well. All right, then. You can call me Kitty Cat."

"Aw, gee *whiz,*" Mike said. "That's just plain *silly.*"

"You *said.*"

"Yes, but gee."

"I always wanted to be a kitty cat," the horse said. "They're so small and everything."

"But you're *not* a kitty cat. What if I wanted to be a horse?"

"I'd call you horsie," the horse said. "I've picked out four names, and you didn't like any of them. I think I'll find another boy."

"Look, I have a good idea," Mike said suddenly. "I have a *great* idea. Your name can be Kitty Cat, just as you said, only we'll call you by your initials, K.C., for short. Like Casey. Get it?"

"No. It's too complicated."

"No, it isn't. It's simple. Casey. I think that's a great name."

12

"Oh, all right," the horse said coldly. "I suppose I can get used to it."

"Come on, Casey, let's go tell my mother,"
Mike said, but Casey had found a new patch of
grass.

"You tell her," Casey said, chewing.

"No, come on, now. You won't know which one is my house or anything."

"All right," Casey said, still chewing.

"Please come on, Casey," Mike begged. Finally Casey followed, and they went down the street to Mike's red house.

## Casey's New Home

Usually when Mike came home from school, he
would throw his lunch box, his sweater, his
baseball cards, and his rocks down on the front
steps. Then his mother would tell him to go out
and get them. But today he brought them all inside because he wanted his mother to let him
keep Casey.

"Mom! Mom!" he called. "We've got a horse! A real live horse! And he can be mine and live in the garage!"

"Hello, dear," Mike's mother said. "Now, go get your—oh, you've brought them in."

"Mom, we have a horse! He's real, and he's going to live with us in the garage."

Mrs. Bradford looked out of the window.

"Why, there *is* a horse out there!" she said in surprise. "For heaven's sake! I wonder where he came from."

"Can we keep him?"

"*Keep* him! Where on earth would we keep a horse?"

"In the garage. We could make him comfortable there."

"Maybe we could make him comfortable," Mrs. Bradford said, "but what would we do with the car?"

"Daddy could leave the car out."

"Mike, I'm sure this horse belongs to someone."

Mike wasn't very worried about this because he didn't think Casey would have been looking for a boy if he already had belonged to someone. So he just said, "Well, if he doesn't belong to anyone, can we keep him?"

"Well, we'll have to talk to Daddy. I'll call

the police and the A.S.P.C.A. and see if they know anything about the horse."

"His name is Casey," Mike said. "If I can keep him, I'll pick up my room every day, and I'll go to bed on time and everything."

"We'll see," his mother said.

Mike could hardly wait until Gloria came home from school. She was in a higher grade and her bus got home later. He ran all the way to the bus stop to meet her. Then he waited for the other children to start home so nobody else would hear the news. Finally he said, "Gloria, guess what?"

"Will you carry some of these books for me, Mike?" she asked.

"Sure. Listen, Gloria, I found a horse, and he can talk, only not to grownups. His name is Casey. It's short for Kitty Cat, and that's silly, but at first he wanted to be called Mike or Gloria or Mr. Bradford. He was at the bus stop, waiting for a boy."

"Jimmy Nichols said his cat can say 'Mama,' only I don't believe it," Gloria said.

"Listen, Gloria, Casey really talks. Mom's going to call to see if he belongs to somebody, but I'm pretty sure he doesn't. And if he doesn't, Dad might let us keep him. Casey is out in the yard now."

"You mean there's a horse at our house right now?"

"Yes. He's waiting for me to come back."

They started walking home as fast as they could. This time, it was Gloria who threw down her books, her lunch box, and her sweater on the front steps.

Casey had gone into the garage.

"Casey," Mike said, "this is my sister Gloria."

Casey didn't say anything. Gloria frowned at Mike.

"Casey, this is Gloria," Mike said again.

Casey didn't say anything. He looked at Gloria and looked away.

"Golly, Casey," Mike said, "this is my sister Gloria. Can't you say something?"

"I *heard* you—it's your sister Gloria, for heaven's sake. What am I supposed to do, ask her to dance or something?"

"You're supposed to say hello when you're introduced to someone."

"Hello," Casey said glumly.

20

"How wonderful!" Gloria said. "Oh, I hope we can keep him!"

"I'm not really crazy about girls," Casey said, looking at Gloria.

"Oh," Gloria said, stepping back a little.

"What I really wanted was a boy," Casey said.

"Well, there's a boy here, so it's all right, isn't it?" Gloria asked.

"I guess so. If you don't mind, I think I'll go out and get a snack." Casey went outside and began to eat grass, while Gloria and Mike watched.

"Casey," Gloria said, "would you mind if I invited some of my friends over?"

"Go ahead," Casey said. "You can have a nice game of dolls. Inside."

"I mean, to see you, Casey."

"I imagine they've all seen a horse before."

"Well, what I really meant was to talk to you."

Casey looked up at Mike. "Girls never say what they really mean, do they? Not until they've said two other things first."

"Well, is it all right?" Gloria asked.

Casey cleared his throat. "I think we'd better straighten this thing out right now," he said. "As you see, I have a new boy. He's a little hard to get along with, but I believe that in time he can be trained to be a fairly good pet. Now, this does not mean that I have to talk talk talk to everyone, does it?"

"No, I guess not," Gloria said timidly.

"All right," Casey said. "As a matter of fact, I have no intention of talking to anyone else at all. It only makes trouble." He ate some more grass, and then he added, "If they want, I'll eat their grass."

"Well, I suppose it's up to you whom you talk to," Gloria said.

"Yes, isn't it?" Casey answered.

"You wouldn't have to talk to them," Mike said. "You could just give rides."

22

Casey looked up. "I beg your pardon?"

"Give rides," Mike said. "Maybe Dad could get hold of a saddle somewhere. Or maybe we could get a little cart, or even a carriage!"

"What for?" Casey asked.

"For the kids to sit in while you pull them around."

"*Pull* them? You actually mean you want me to pull around a cart full of children?"

"Well," Mike said, "something like that. It would sure be fun!"

"Who would it be fun for?" Casey asked.

"Well, them."

"Exactly. Them."

"Wouldn't it make you happy to see all the children having such a good time?" Gloria asked.

Casey turned to Mike. "Do you like girls?" he asked.

Mike didn't know what to say.

Then Casey turned to Gloria. "Gloria," he

24

said, "how could I possibly see the children having a good time if I was in front of them pulling a cart? Hm? You can't put the cart before the horse, you know."

"But you'd *know* they were having a good time," Gloria said. "Wouldn't that make you happy?"

"No," Casey said.

"We could still get a saddle, and you could give plain rides on your back," Mike said. "That would be easy for you."

"How would you like a bunch of strangers having plain rides on your back?" Casey asked.

"That's different," Mike said. "I'm no horse."

"If you were, you'd have more horse sense, obviously," Casey said.

"But Casey," Mike said, "other horses give rides. They don't think a thing of it."

"Where?" Casey asked, looking around. "I don't see a single one."

"I mean other horses in other places."

"Then that doesn't help a bit, does it?" Casey asked. He began to eat grass again.

Mike and Gloria sighed. "Well, anyway," Gloria said to Mike, "we have a wonderful horse, and he talks to us, and that's more than most other kids have."

"I have a talking boy who has a talking sister," Casey said. "Now, why don't you two go talk to each other a while and let me eat in peace?"

## "*Do You Like Girls?*"

That night, Mike and Gloria could hardly wait for their father to come home. As soon as he came inside the house, Mike began to bounce up and down saying, "Dad, can we keep Casey? You don't mind leaving the car out, do you? Is it all right?"

27

And at the same time, Gloria was saying, "Be quiet, Mike! Let me tell it! Stop bouncing!"

Finally, their mother came out of the kitchen and took off her apron.

"What's all this about?" Mr. Bradford asked.

"Oh, a stray horse came by here today, and I've called everywhere, but nobody seems to know where he came from or what to do with him. The children are having a fit, as you can see. They're dying to keep him in the garage."

Mr. Bradford laughed. "Let's have a look," he said. They all went out to the garage. Mr. Bradford patted Casey and said, "Hi, fellow. You're a pretty good looking horse. Maybe you'll eat our grass and save me the trouble of mowing it."

Mike and Gloria started talking at once again, and when they got back inside, Mr. Bradford said, "If you two will calm down a minute, maybe we can decide what to do."

The children stopped talking, and he went on,

"Now, I'm sure someone will claim this horse. But in the meantime, it will be all right if you keep him in the garage." He turned to their mother. "That all right with you?"

"I guess so," she said.

Mike said, "Hooray!" And Gloria said, "Oh, *thank* you!" And after dinner they all went out to the garage to make sure Casey would be comfortable for the night.

The next day was Saturday, the day Mrs. Bradford went to do her marketing. Mike decided to go with her.

First, he opened the box that his sneakers came in because that was where his money was. He tied all his money into a red scarf and fastened it onto his belt. Then he was ready to go. He wanted to buy some sugar in lumps for Casey.

It was hard to find the sugar in lumps in the store, because the boxes were up high, and he

had to ask a man in a white apron to get a box down for him. Then he couldn't find his mother for a while, and he got sort of worried. Finally he saw her where the lettuce was, and when she was finished, they drove home.

Mike could hardly wait to get out of the car. He ran into the garage and shouted, "Look, Casey, I brought you a surprise! Which hand?"

"I don't want it," Casey said.

"You will when you see it." Mike smiled a

big smile and held out the sugar. "Look," he said.

"Oh," Casey said, turning away. "Do I *have* to eat it?"

"What do you mean?" Mike asked. "It's *sugar!*"

"I *hate* sugar," Casey said.

"You *couldn't* hate sugar," Mike said, beginning to feel a little angry. "Have you ever had any?"

"No. But I know I hate it."

"Listen," Mike said, and he was pretty mad now, "listen, I went all the way to the super market, and I spent my own money, and gee, everybody loves sugar. Especially every horse. Won't you at least try it?"

"Well, I'll take a little taste," Casey said. Mike gave him a lump. Casey tried to bite it in two, so he wouldn't have to take such a big taste. The lump fell on the floor and broke.

"Oh, my gosh, take the whole thing," Mike said disgustedly. Casey took a broken half.

"Do you like it?" Mike asked.

"I guess it's all right."

"Do you want more?"

"Well, a couple of lumps, I guess." Mike gave him a few lumps. "It's not too bad, actually," Casey said. "You may as well give me the rest of the box."

"Hey, you can't eat it all in one day," Mike said.

"Why not?"

"Because! Well, for one thing, you wouldn't have any tomorrow."

"But I don't want it tomorrow. I want it right now."

"But when it *is* tomorrow, you'll want it then!"

"Well then," Casey said, "you can buy me another box tomorrow."

"I can't either," Mike said. "I don't have any more money."

"Ask your mother for money to buy more."

"Listen, I had a hard enough time convincing her to keep you."

"I can go right now, if I'm such a bother," Casey said.

"Oh, come on, Casey, don't go."

"I don't think you're a bit nice," Casey said, and he stamped his foot.

"Hey, watch it with that foot, you big horse," Mike said. "You almost stepped on me."

"I think you're *mean,*" Casey said, turning his head away.

"Gee whiz, Casey, you just don't understand," Mike said, and he sat down on a big wooden box. He didn't know what to do. For a long time he just sat there looking at Casey, and Casey just stood there.

Finally, Casey said softly, "I know what I *would* like."

"What?" Mike asked eagerly.

"I'd *really* like some striped pajamas."

"Good grief, Casey. Horses don't wear pajamas."

"Have you ever seen a horse in pajamas?" Casey asked.

"Of course not."

"Then how do you know?"

"How do I know what?" Mike asked. "I don't get it."

"I never had a pair of striped pajamas in my whole life," Casey said. A big tear fell on the old Army blanket Mike had put on the floor. "You *never* do *anything* I want." Another tear fell.

"Casey, there just aren't any pajamas for horses."

"You're mean," Casey said, turning his head away.

"Where in the world would I ever get any pajamas that would fit you?" Mike asked.

"How should I know?"

"Listen," Mike said, "listen, Casey, maybe Gloria could make you some. She made eight aprons last Christmas, I know that. Maybe she could make you some striped pajamas."

"Could she? Could she really?"

"Well, I can ask her," Mike said, and he ran inside to get Gloria.

Gloria always cleaned her room on Saturday mornings, and now she was just finishing. Mike sat down on the edge of her bed and said, "Listen, Gloria, Casey wants you to make him some striped pajamas."

"Oh, for Pete's sake," Gloria said.

"No, listen, he's *crying,* and he said he might leave."

"Well, just explain to him that horses never wear any pajamas at all."

"I did, but it didn't do any good," Mike said.

"Well, I can try talking to him," Gloria said.
"But you know how he is about girls."

They went out to the garage together. Casey
smiled when he saw Gloria.

"I think it's perfectly grand of you to make me striped pajamas, Gloria," Casey said. "Mike told me you would."

"I did not," Mike said.

"Listen, Casey," Gloria said, "I don't know how to make pajamas. And it would take so much material. Where would I get all that material?"

"You could buy it," Casey said.

"I don't have the money to buy it," Gloria said. "I mean, I'm saving up for a certain record, and that will take another week's allowance. Then I think it would take about another month after that to save up for that much striped material, not even counting buttons and thread and everything."

"Talk talk talk," Casey said. "I've never had any pajamas in my whole life, and you don't even *care.*"

"Gosh, Casey, it isn't that," she said, and she gave Mike a worried look. "Do you know what?

I could make you a thing like . . ." She looked
at Casey closely. "Well, sort of like an apron,
only a little more like a saddle type of thing. I
don't mind waiting another week to get that
record. I could get some striped material and
make you this darling little thing. Wouldn't you
like that, Casey?"

"I don't want a *thing*," Casey said. "I want
striped pajamas."

He began to cry. He turned his back on Mike
and Gloria and started bumping his head
against the lawn mower.

"Hey, don't fool with Dad's mower," Mike
said, but Casey bumped even harder. "Casey,
cut it out," Mike said.

"Why can't I have the striped pajamas?"
Casey asked, snuffling and bumping. Mike
looked at Gloria.

"Oh, all right, I'll *try*," Gloria said. "But I
don't think they'll be very good."

"Oh gee, thanks, Gloria," Casey said. He

turned around and rubbed his nose against her
cheek.

"I don't know when I'll get my record," Gloria said. "And I can tell you, Casey, you're going to look pretty silly."

But Casey just smiled.

The next chance they got, Mike and Gloria
went downtown with Gloria's record money.

"I wonder what color would look nice on Casey," Gloria said. "Do you think orange stripes would be nice?"

"Great," Mike said. "Blue would look good, too."

Finally, they picked out some orange striped material.

When they got back home again, their mother

said she didn't know where they got such a silly idea, but she let Gloria take some buttons of hers, and Gloria started making the pajamas. Every day she took the big bundle of material out to the garage and tried to fit it onto Casey, and it was a pretty hard job.

Right away, a little girl came up and said, "Oh, Gloria, what are you doing *that* for?" And when Gloria told her, she went running to look for her sister, calling, "Jean, Jean, come quick. Gloria Bradford's making striped pajamas for a *horse!*"

Pretty soon, all the children in the neighborhood came to watch.

"Why do you want to put pajamas on him?" a boy asked.

Mike could tell Gloria was a little embarrassed, but she smiled and said, "Oh, we just thought it would be different."

Someone else said, "Hey, Gloria, when you get through with the pajamas, why don't you make him a bathrobe?"

Finally, Gloria finished the striped pajamas, and Casey was very happy. He didn't even want to take them off to be washed. After a few days, Casey had the pajamas on so much it was hard for Mike to remember how he'd looked without them.

## The Uninvited Guest

One afternoon, Mike said, "Casey, I'm going
to a birthday party down at Billy Brant's house.
I'll be back after a while."

"Will you have cake and hats and balloons?"

"Sure," Mike said.

"Nothing's more fun than a birthday party,"
Casey said pleasantly.

Mike was surprised that Casey didn't make
a fuss, but he was glad, too. He went inside and

washed part of his face and hands and put on the clothes his mother had told him to wear: the scratchy trousers, the shirt that made his neck feel funny, and the brown corduroy jacket. Then he took the present his mother had wrapped and walked down to Billy Brant's house.

The party was in the back yard. There was a picnic table with a paper tablecloth on it, and little baskets and hats. Mr. and Mrs. Brant were there, and Billy was showing everyone the new scooter they had given him.

Mike went over to Billy and handed him the present and said, "Here." Then he remembered and said, "Happy Birthday."

Billy said, "Put it on the table." Then *he* remembered and said, "Thanks."

Billy unwrapped his presents and let some of the boys try on his new holster, and two of the children played with a toy golf set.

Mike was taking a turn on the new scooter

when, suddenly, Mrs. Brant cried, "Oh, look!"

Everyone looked, and there was Casey, coming around the side of the house in his striped pajamas.

"Oh, George, look at that darling horse!" Mrs. Brant called excitedly to Mr. Brant. "Get your camera. Have you ever seen such a thing?"

All the children laughed, and Mike said, "That's my horse, Casey."

"Casey wanted to come to the party," Mrs. Brant said. "George, take a picture of him with the children."

"May we ride him?" someone asked.

"I don't think Casey would like that," Mike said.

"We can play pin-the-tail on the horse, instead of pin-the-tail on the donkey."

"I don't think Casey would like that, either," Mike said.

"Well, what *would* Casey like?" Billy asked.

Casey bent down and whispered very softly in Mike's ear so that nobody else could hear.

"Oh, isn't that the cutest thing," Mrs. Brant said. "That horse is kissing Mike's ear!"

"I guess he'd like a hat," Mike said.

"What a wonderful idea!" said Mrs. Brant. She picked out a straw hat and put it on Casey. "Isn't that a scream? Are you taking pictures,

George? Where did he get the striped pajamas?"

"My sister made them," Mike said. He felt very silly.

"You'd swear he was smiling," Mr. Brant said, taking pictures. The children were all laughing and patting Casey and running around.

"He certainly is good natured, isn't he?" Mr. Brant said to Mike.

"Well, sort of," Mike replied.

Casey whispered in Mike's ear again, and Mike said, "Maybe Casey would like a balloon."

"Let's give him a red one," Billy said. "Where shall we put it?"

Mike was embarrassed, but Casey was looking at him, so he said, "Maybe we could tie it onto his tail."

They tied a red balloon to the top of his tail, and the children were laughing so loud that Mrs. Brant had to call lots of times before they would all sit down to eat. Casey followed them to the table and stood next to Mike.

"Do you think Casey would like something
to eat?" Mrs. Brant asked. "What should we
give him?"

Casey whispered to Mike again. "I think,"
Mike said uncomfortably, "he would like a pea-
nut butter sandwich, two carrot sticks, and a
piece of cake."

When it was time to go, everyone said good-
bye to Casey, and two of the girls kissed him on
the neck.

After they got back to the garage, Mike said,
"Casey, I wish you wouldn't do that again."

"Don't be silly," Casey said. "They thought
I was adorable."

"I don't like them thinking I made up all
those silly things, like the hat and the balloon."

"Oh, don't be ridiculous. They loved it."

"And another thing," Mike said. "You
shouldn't have eaten all that stuff. Why can't
you eat like a horse?"

"Why Mike, I'm surprised at you," Casey said. "That would have been very rude."

"Anyway, please don't do it again," Mike said.

"I really don't understand what you mean," Casey said, "but I hope you'll stop fussing. It's a bad habit of yours."

Mike looked at Casey. He couldn't think of anything to say, so he went back inside and changed into his blue jeans.

## Headlines

A few days later, Mike went out to see Casey after school and said, "I won't be here tomorrow afternoon, Casey. It's a special day. My mother promised me a chocolate sundae because I did my jobs for two weeks, so she's going to drive me downtown tomorrow afternoon and we're going to the drugstore. After that we're going to the five and ten, and I get to pick out a whole dollar's worth of toys because my aunt sent me a dollar for writing her such a nice letter. And, after that, we're meeting Daddy, and our whole family's going to my grandmother's for dinner."

"That sounds very nice," Casey said. "I'll come along."

"Gosh, I'm sorry, but Grandma didn't invite you," Mike said.

"Oh," Casey said. "Well, I guess I can understand that. I mean, your grandmother doesn't know me or anything."

"No, she doesn't," Mike said. He was glad Casey wasn't going to make a fuss.

Mike swung his foot and started to think about what he was going to buy with his dollar. He knew he was going to get some marbles and a harmonica and a little wooden airplane and some bubble gum. He'd decided that in school. But he'd still have fifty cents left, and he didn't know whether to buy one big thing or some little ones. And he wasn't *absolutely* sure about the harmonica and the marbles and the airplane because he *might* get a football, which cost ninety-eight cents, and then he would just get two pieces of bubble gum, one for Gloria and one for himself.

"I'll come back home before dinner," Casey said.

"What?"

"I'll just have the sundae with you, and then come home by myself."

"Oh," Mike said, and he began to get the feeling he was going to have some trouble. "Look, Casey, I'm sorry, but horses just don't go in drugstores, and that's all there is to it."

"Have you ever seen a horse—"

"No!" Mike said. "Now don't start *that* stuff. I'm telling you, horses don't. You'll just have to believe me. I've been in drugstores lots of times and I know. I'm sorry."

"I've never had a sundae," Casey said sadly.

"Listen, Casey, we couldn't even *get* to the drugstore. It's downtown, and we couldn't walk because my mother wants me to go with her in the car, and it's pretty far, and you couldn't get into the car."

"I could too."

"No you couldn't, Casey. There are some things you're just the wrong size for. I know you couldn't get into the car. There are special trucks for moving horses. They're called horse trailers. Why do you think they use those?"

"Why?"

"Because horses can't get in regular cars, stupid."

Casey turned away.

"OK, I'm sorry I called you stupid," Mike said. He wondered if Casey were going to start crying, or bumping the lawn mower, or saying he wanted to find another boy. But he didn't say anything, and Mike felt pretty bad.

Just then Gloria came in. She was carrying a newspaper, and she was all excited.

"Guess what?" she said. "Mrs. Brant sent some of those pictures of the birthday party in to the newspaper, and here they are! There's a big picture of Casey, and you're in it, too, Mike, and so is Billy Brant."

"Let's see," Casey said. "Well, imagine that! There I am in the straw hat. It's quite a good picture, isn't it?"

"You can hardly tell it's me," Mike said. "You can't tell the pajamas are striped either."

"Let's see it again," Casey said. "My, it certainly is a fine picture, especially of me. Read what it says, Gloria."

"It says, 'Mr. and Mrs. George Brant of 43 Spruce Lane' . . ."

"No, no. Not that part. Read what it says about me."

"I was getting to that. Now, where was I? Oh! '. . . gave a birthday party for their son Billy on Saturday'—"

"Skip that part," Casey said. "All I want to hear is the part about me."

"I'll get to it. Give me a chance," Gloria said.

Casey turned to Mike. "Do you like girls?" Then Mike's mother called him, and he was glad he didn't have to answer that question again. There was a telephone call, his mother said.

A man on the telephone said, "Is this Mike Bradford?"

Mike said that he was, and the man explained that he was the high school dramatics teacher, and that he needed a horse for a school play. He said he'd seen Casey's picture in the paper that morning, and wondered if they could use him. Mike asked what Casey would do in the play, and the dramatics teacher said all Casey would have to do was to walk onstage in the last scene, carrying the king and followed by knights in armor. Mike took the man's telephone number and said he'd call him back. Then he went back to the garage.

"I know you won't want to do it," he said, "but the high school dramatics teacher saw your picture in the paper and wants you to be in a high school play. I'm supposed to call him back and give him the answer. I guess there must not be any other horses right around here."

"A play?" Casey asked. "I've never been in a play. I'm not at all sure I'd like it."

"Well, I'm sure you wouldn't," Mike said. "You'd have to stand on the stage, carrying the king, followed by knights in armor."

"The king, you say? Followed by knights in armor? Well!"

"Not a real king or knights, of course. It would just be high school kids in a play," Gloria said.

"A king," Casey said dreamily. "The king's royal horse. I might be willing to help them out, at that."

"Casey," Gloria said, "it might be *work*. I mean, there will probably be rehearsals and all."

"I'd be up on the stage, did you say? All the people would be looking at me. They'd probably clap for me. I believe my answer will be yes. After all, one has to cooperate with others, hasn't one?"

For a minute, nobody said anything. Then Mike said, "Casey, about going to the drugstore tomorrow afternoon—"

"Never mind that," Casey said. "When is this play?"

"He didn't say."

"You'd better ask him when you call," Casey said. "You'd better call him right away."

"O.K.," Mike said, and he went into the house to make the call.

"I wonder if I'll have a very nice costume," Casey said. "What do you suppose royal horses wear?"

"Probably just some kind of fancy saddle," Gloria said.

"A fancy saddle," Casey said. "My!"

After a few minutes Mike came out again and told Casey that the play was two weeks off, and he'd only have to go to one rehearsal, the dress rehearsal Saturday afternoon. The play was Saturday night. Casey seemed very pleased.

"The man didn't mention what kind of costume I'd have?" Casey asked.

"No, he didn't say anything about that."

"Oh. You should have asked."

"Casey, there's something else. I didn't ask

you, because I was sure you wouldn't want to do it, but there's a pet show tomorrow morning at the ball field. If you don't mind being in the play, maybe you wouldn't mind—"

"You want me to enter you in the pet show, don't you?" Casey asked kindly. "Why, of *course* I will. I can't imagine that you would win any prizes, but it's nice harmless fun." He smiled.

"Well, what I meant was that *I* would enter *you* in the pet show," Mike said. But Casey wasn't listening.

"I believe I'll wear my hat and balloon, besides the pajamas. One has to be presentable in crowds."

"Oh, you don't have to do that," Mike said quickly. "I mean, wear any old thing. Like—nothing at all."

"My dear boy, *what* a suggestion! I wouldn't dream of it. And you'd better get me some dark glasses."

"Dark glasses? What for?"

"So nobody will know who I am, naturally. Now that I'm famous, with my picture in the paper and everything, people might recognize me. I wouldn't want to take any attention away from you."

"I'm really not too crazy about pet shows," Mike said. "It wasn't such a great idea after all. Let's not go."

"Of *course* we'll go," Casey said grandly, and he wouldn't talk about it any more.

## A Pet Among Pets

The next morning, Casey was still determined to take Mike to the pet show. Mike had to dress him in his pajamas, his hat, his balloon, and the dark glasses Mike had borrowed from his father. Mike wished he had never started the whole business. Everyone would think it was his idea to dress up his horse like this to be cute or

something, and Mike didn't think it was cute at all. He thought it was the silliest thing he'd ever seen, and he wished it would start to rain so they could go back home. But it was a very sunny day, and no matter how slowly they walked, they were sure to get there sooner or later.

As they approached the ball field, Mike began to think it would have been better to get there early if they had to go at all, because now the crowd had gathered and everybody began to notice Casey. Long before Mike and Casey got

to the line of pets, people had begun to laugh
and shout and point at Casey. Then a whole lot
of people started running up to them.

"I'm afraid they *do* recognize me, in spite of
the dark glasses," Casey said cheerfully.

"Yes," Mike said unhappily.

"Well, never mind," said Casey. "At least
they'll have to look at you. Now Mike, you
mustn't feel too bad if you don't win any prizes.
Boys are very common. Good heavens, what are
those awful little brown things?"

"Dogs," Mike said. "They're called Pekinese. I know, because they won prizes last year and the year before."

"You mean people actually keep those things as pets?" Casey asked. "In that case, perhaps you *do* have a chance. The pet selection must be very poor."

"We'll just have to wait and see," Mike said miserably.

The people were crowding close now, laughing, shouting, and asking Mike questions.

"Does he do tricks?"

"Where'd he get the pajamas?"

"Where did you get him?"

"What's his name?"

Mike tried to answer politely, but it was hard because he felt so silly.

It took them a long time to get into line with the other pets because there were so many people around them.

The Pekinese dogs suddenly saw Casey, and

they began to bark and growl. They broke away from the girl who was holding them, and she had to run all over the ball field before she could catch them. When the girl finally got back in line with the dogs, she was all out of breath. She turned to Mike and said, "If dressing a horse all up in fancy clothes is your idea of a joke, I don't think it's one bit funny."

"I don't either," Mike said.

When almost everyone was lined up, the judging started. A few of the judges had to chase some of the pets because there was so much commotion over Casey. The judge announced the prizes for the Best Looking, the Best Trained, and the Best of Kind. Then he smiled and said that there was no doubt among the judges about which was the Most Unusual Pet.

In a few minutes a man came over and shook Mike's hand and hung a wreath of flowers around Casey's neck. Everyone clapped and shouted and whistled then, and it was all over.

It took a long time to get out of the ball field because of the crowd, and then once they were on the road, people in cars honked and yelled at them.

At last, they got back home. "There now," Casey said, "aren't you glad you went after all?"

"I guess so," Mike said, but he didn't sound as if he meant it.

"I'm very proud of you for winning a prize, Mike. It's no wonder. You were the most un-usual."

"What do you mean?"

"Didn't you see? There wasn't one other boy in the contest," Casey said.

## Enter Casey On Stage

Later on that morning, Casey said, "I'm afraid I'm not going to have as much time as I usually have for you from now on, Mike."

"Why is that?" Mike asked.

"I'm going to be busy. I have to get into condition for the play."

"What kind of condition do you have to get into?" Mike asked.

"Into *good* condition, of course," Casey said irritably.

"Oh," Mike said. "Well, how are you going to do it?"

"Exercise, naturally," Casey said.

"You have to exercise to walk across a stage?" Mike asked.

"Apparently you don't have the slightest understanding of show business," Casey said. "Entertainers have to work very hard. They have to stay in good shape."

"Oh," Mike said. "You're in bad shape?"

"For heaven's sake. There you go, being unreasonable again. All I said was that I thought I'd get a little exercise. What I had in mind was running around the block a few times every morning."

"In your pajamas?"

"Of course."

"And your hat, and balloon, and dark glasses, and paper flowers?"

"Certainly. Unless, of course, you plan to provide a more suitable outfit."

"Don't you think you could just run around the yard, if you have to run?"

"You're not using your head today," Casey said. "Anyone can see the yard is too small."

"I don't know how the neighbors will feel. People don't like to have horses running around their houses and up and down the street."

"Oh, don't be silly. People think I'm terrific. Can't you tell?"

"Well, they certainly do notice you," Mike said.

"As long as I'm dressed, I may as well go now," Casey said. With no further warning, he was off, clippity-clop, down the street.

"Hey, come back!" Mike called. But Casey kept on running, and soon he was out of sight around the corner.

Gloria came out of the house. She'd been cleaning her room again.

"How was the pet show?" she asked.

"Fine," Mike said glumly. "He won a string of paper flowers. He has them around his neck. He scared two dogs, and the girl had to run all over to get them. Everyone was laughing at us, too."

"Where is he now?"

"He's running around the block. He says he needs to get into condition to be in the play."

"Running around the block! Oh, dear," Gloria said.

"And he's wearing all his stuff, too."

"Oh, dear," Gloria said again.

They sat quietly for a while, and then they heard Casey pounding down the street. He ran into their driveway and whinnied importantly. "Hello, Gloria," he panted. "My, there's nothing like a little exercise. Did you hear that Mike won a prize as the Most Unusual Pet?"

"He told me."

"It's no wonder," Casey said. "You should have seen some of the peculiar creatures that were entered."

Just then Mike's mother came out of the house looking worried.

"Is Casey here? Oh, yes, I see he is. Thank goodness! You children must tie him up right away and not let him run any more."

"How did you know he was running?" Mike asked.

"I'll tell you how I knew," Mrs. Bradford said. "First, Mrs. Elliot telephoned. Mrs. Elliot's old mother is visiting. She hadn't heard about Casey, and when the poor lady looked out the kitchen window and saw a horse in striped pajamas gallop by she fainted, right then and there. Then Mrs. Harris called. She said that her baby was on the porch in a play pen when Casey came dashing by, and the baby started to scream and hasn't stopped yet. Then, Mrs. Riley called. She said she was bringing in the milk when she saw that crazy horse she'd been hearing about, all dressed up in fancy clothes. She was so startled she dropped the milk, and all four bottles broke in the driveway. She said she was going to call the police." Mrs. Bradford took a deep breath. "And then the police called. They asked us to tie up the horse."

"Oh," Mike said.

"Oh," Gloria said.

Mrs. Bradford went back inside the house.

"Well, I guess you heard what she said," Mike said.

"I heard," Casey said. "I don't know what all the fuss is about. Heavens, you'd think I was a dragon! Oh well, I'm not worried. When they realize how famous I'm becoming, it will be a different story, you wait and see."

## *The Star*

At last the day of the play came. Mike went out
to talk to Casey before the high school boys
came to pick him up. "I hope you won't be disappointed," he said.

"What is there to be disappointed about?"
Casey asked. "I'm just doing them a favor."

"You know, you'll have to leave your pajamas and all the rest of your stuff at home."

"Why, of course! They'll have a special costume for me."

"Maybe," Mike said. He sat on the wooden box, swinging his legs. He was a little worried about Casey and the play.

"You *are* coming to the play, aren't you?" Casey asked.

"Sure," Mike said. "We wouldn't miss it for anything. Mother said she would take Gloria and me. Casey, you know they can't bring you back home until tomorrow."

"That's perfectly all right," Casey said. "I understand about those things."

Then a truck pulled up, and two boys came to take Casey over to the high school. That afternoon, Mr. Bradford said it was nice to put the car in the garage again, and Mrs. Bradford said it was nice not to have to worry about the

police or the neighbors calling. Gloria and Mike didn't say anything.

After dinner, Mike and Gloria dressed up in their uncomfortable clothes and Mrs. Bradford drove them to the high school.

The play wasn't too bad, Mike thought. There were some parts he didn't understand, but everyone laughed, so he did, too. He hadn't

expected it to be a funny play because you don't think of kings and knights being in funny plays, but this one was.

Mike didn't count on seeing Casey on the stage until the last scene because that was what the dramatics teacher had said, so he was quite surprised when Casey walked on much earlier.

One of the actors said to Casey, "Noble steed, who is the greatest king on earth?" And Casey

bowed down before the court jester, who was supposed to be something like a clown. Everyone laughed and laughed. Then when Casey came on the stage later, he bowed to the audience, and they all cheered and clapped.

"Did you children know Casey could do that trick?" Mrs. Bradford asked.

"Not exactly," Gloria said.

"I wasn't too surprised, though," Mike said.

"He must be easily trained," their mother said.

Mike and Gloria wanted to go backstage to see Casey, but Mrs. Bradford said it was late, and, besides, they'd see him the next morning.

Mike slept much later than usual the next morning, and by the time he got up the boys had already brought Casey back. Mike went right out to the garage to talk to him.

"Did you see me, Mike?" Casey asked excitedly. "Did you see me up there on the stage?"

"Sure I did. I told you we were going."

"A man was talking about me at the rehearsal," Casey said. "He said I must have been trained." He paused a moment, as though he were going to say something else. Then he asked, "Did Gloria think I was good?"

"Sure she did. We all did."

"Did she say so? Were people talking about me?"

"I guess so," Mike said. "I didn't hear too

much about what people were saying because we had to come right home afterward. It was pretty late."

"Did you hear them clapping for me?" Casey asked.

"Sure we heard them."

"They clapped and clapped. It was a very funny play. I'm a steed in the play. Doesn't that sound nice? It means horse. There's this king, and—"

"I *know,* Casey. We were *there.*"

"Wasn't it funny, especially when I bowed to that court jester?"

"Yes," Mike said. He was getting a little tired of hearing about the play. "Well, I'm glad you had such a good time. Listen, Casey, is it all right with you if I go down and play with Billy a while?"

"Go ahead," Casey said, and Mike started to go. "They certainly did like me, didn't they?" Casey called.

"Yes," Mike said, and he ran out quickly. He went to Billy's house. First they wrestled, then they played cowboys, and then they looked for rocks. He had a very good time.

When he was walking home, Mike thought that he really hadn't played much with his friends for quite a while, ever since he'd had Casey.

## Grand Exit

When he got home, a man was just leaving in
his car, and Mike's father was standing out on
the front steps.

"Mike, I want to talk to you," he said. Mike
wondered what was wrong because his father
looked so serious. They went inside and sat
down.

"Mike," he said, "that man was here to talk about Casey. He thinks he's an unusual horse."

"I think he's an unusual horse, too," Mike said.

"He seems to think Casey has possibilities as a circus horse. Now, I know you and Gloria are very fond of Casey. But you haven't had much time for anything else since he came. You hardly see your friends any more, do you?"

"Well, not much," Mike admitted.

"I don't think you've been over to the ball field for the games at all since he came, or to the library, have you?" Mike shook his head. "You see, when Casey first came, your mother and I never imagined it would be for so long. When the weather gets colder, it will be important to put the car in the garage, too. You do understand that, don't you?"

"Sure," Mike said. "I think Casey would be a good circus horse."

"Then you won't mind? It sounded like a

good idea to me. I hope it isn't too much of a disappointment for you."

"It's O.K. with me," Mike said.

Mr. Bradford went on talking. He was talking about how they didn't really have a comfortable place for Casey, and how a horse should have room to run.

But Mike wasn't listening very closely because he was thinking about how he was going to tell Casey. Mike understood now that Casey thought of him as a pet boy, and since he had always wanted a pet boy, Mike could just imagine the fuss Casey would make about going away.

When his father got through talking, Mike went right out to see Casey.

"Casey," he said, "I have to talk to you."

"First," Casey said, "I have something to tell you. You won't like it."

"What is it?"

"I hate to say it," Casey said, hanging his

head. "I just know you'll make a terrible fuss."

"Well, go ahead and say it anyway."

"Well," Casey said, taking a deep breath, "when the dramatics teacher and a friend of his were talking about me at the rehearsal—you know, saying how I could do tricks and how easy it would be to train me and all—they said something else. I should have told you right away, but I just couldn't. I knew it would make you feel awful."

"Oh," Mike said. He smiled. He wasn't going to have to break the news to Casey. Casey was going to break it to him instead.

"What they said was—well, you see, a friend of the dramatics teacher is with a circus. He wants me in it." Casey looked up. "I feel awful about it, of course, but I think I should go. So, when he calls, will you tell him I'll go?"

"Sure, Casey, I'll tell him. I think you'd be good in a circus."

"But you won't be anyone's pet any more.

You won't have anyone to talk to, and there'll be nobody living in the garage. It will be empty. Except for the car." Casey cried a little.

"That's all right," Mike said. "Think what fun you'll have in the circus."

"Oh, *yes,*" Casey said, and his tears were suddenly gone. "I'll bet I'll be better than the other horses they have."

"There's no other horse like you, Casey," Mike said. "I'm sure of that."

"That's what I thought," Casey said. "Still, it's too bad you won't be anyone's pet."

"Well, don't you worry about it," Mike said. "You'll be swell in the circus."

After a few days, Casey left. Two men came to get him, and, as he stepped happily into the truck, he turned and winked at Mike and Gloria.

Mike and Gloria cleaned the garage, and their father put the car back in. Then the two children sat on the front steps.

"Golly, I'll sure miss Casey," Mike said. "I guess every kid in the world wants a horse. I guess any kid would sure miss him when he left."

"Oh, yes," Gloria said. "I just don't know what we'll do without him. Golly, we can do anything we want today, can't we?"

"Yes, play with our friends or anything."

"And we can do what we want with our allowances," Gloria said. "We don't have to spend it all on sugar or material for pajamas."

"I'll miss Casey all right," Mike said. "I mean, in some ways, like . . ."

"Oh, I'll miss him, too," Gloria said. "Sometimes, like when . . ."

Then Gloria looked at Mike, and Mike looked at Gloria. Gloria started to giggle a little, and Mike chuckled, and then Gloria laughed, and then Mike laughed. And they laughed until they were all laughed out.